For Georgie, Bethany
and Jemma ~ G. L.

Thanks to Mom, Dad, friends and
myriad family. For Brianna, Isabelle, Gabrielle,
Charlotte, Helena, Amy, Rachel,
Tim and Ange ~ L. H.

Copyright © 2006 by Good Books, Intercourse, PA 17534
International Standard Book Number: 978-1-56148-534-5; 1-56148-534-9
Library of Congress Catalog Card Number: 2006002071

Text copyright © Gill Lewis 2006
Illustrations copyright © Louise Ho 2006

Original edition published in English by Little Tiger Press, an imprint of
Magi Publications, London, England, 2006.

Printed in Singapore by Tien Wah Press Pte.

Library of Congress Cataloging-in-Publication Data

Lewis, Gill.
The most precious thing / Gill Lewis ; illustrated by Louise Ho.
p. cm.
Summary: Little Bear and Mommy Bear explore the many wonders in the
forest, but with each find, Mommy Bear assures Little Bear that there is still
one thing that is more precious than all the others.
ISBN-13: 978-1-56148-534-5 (hardcover)
[1. Mother and child--Fiction. 2. Bears--Fiction.]   I. Ho, Louise, ill. II. Title.

PZ7.L58537Mo 2006
[E]--dc22
2006002071

The Most Precious Thing

Gill Lewis

Illustrated by Louise Ho

Intercourse, PA 17534
800/762-7171
www.GoodBks.com

Little Bear was taking Mommy Bear on a walk through the forest in the autumn sunlight. She wanted to show her the special place where the juiciest berries and the sweetest nuts could be found.

As Little Bear skipped through
the rustling leaves, she suddenly
spied a small blue stone glittering
in the sunshine.

"Look, Mommy, look!" cried Little Bear, picking it up. "Look at this shiny jewel I have found." Little Bear gazed as it sparkled in her paw. "It must be the most precious thing in the whole wide world," she gasped.

"Oh yes, Little Bear, this is a very beautiful stone," said Mommy Bear, holding it up so that it twinkled in the light, "but the most precious thing is even prettier than this."

"Really?" said Little Bear in wonder. She put the stone carefully in her bag. "Let's go and look! I want to find the most precious thing *ever*!"

"Wait for me," laughed Mommy Bear, as Little Bear scampered off through the trees.

Little Bear and Mommy Bear played games
in the afternoon sun. They tried to catch the
seeds that spun in the breeze. And Little Bear
kept looking for something prettier than the
little blue stone.

After a while they came to Little Bear's special place and they filled their tummies with juicy purple blackberries. Little Bear was reaching for a berry when she saw something pink hidden in the brambles . . .

It was a beautiful wild rose.

"Mommy!" shouted Little Bear excitedly. "Come and see what I have found!"

She stroked the rose's silky petals and sniffed its sweet smell. "I've never seen such a pretty flower. Surely this must be the most precious thing?"

"This rose is very pretty, Little Bear," said Mommy Bear, "and it's soft as velvet." She tickled the rose against Little Bear's nose, making her sneeze. "But the most precious thing is even softer than this."

Little Bear wondered what on earth could be softer than her beautiful rose. She searched and searched through the dry, crunchy leaves, but she found only spiky horse chestnuts, bristly pine cones and a rather cross hedgehog.

Just then she caught sight of something fluttering high up in the trees.

"Look up there, Mommy!" she shouted. "That *has* to be it!"

Mommy Bear lifted Little Bear up into the air. Caught in a spider's web was a tiny fluffy feather. Little Bear reached up high and took the feather very gently in her paw.

Little Bear touched the downy feather against her cheek.

"Oh Mommy," she whispered hopefully. "Please tell me. Is *this* the most precious thing?"

"It is very soft," said Mommy Bear, "but the most precious thing is even better than this – it makes me want to dance for joy."

And Mommy Bear twirled Little Bear around, making her giggle.

Little Bear was determined to find the most precious thing. She ran up a grassy hilltop to look out at the woods and fields. Hundreds of dazzling butterflies suddenly filled the air around her.

One of the butterflies landed lightly on her paw. Little Bear gazed at it in wonder.

"This is it!" she sang out happily. "At last I have found the most precious thing in the whole of the big wide world."

Little Bear and Mommy Bear lay in the long grass as the butterfly fluttered through the golden sunlight.

"Oh yes, that is very special," said Mommy Bear softly, "but I can hold the most precious thing safe and tight in my arms."

"Oh, please tell me what it is!" said Little Bear impatiently. "I have looked absolutely everywhere and I still haven't found it."

Mommy Bear smiled. "The most precious thing is prettier than any jewel, is softer than a rose or the fluffiest feather, and fills me with more joy than a dancing butterfly. The most precious thing . . ." she said, hugging Little Bear tightly, ". . . is you!"